# Ted works on Apple Tree Farm.

He has just bought a sheepdog to help him with the sheep. The sheepdog is called Patch.

3

Poppy, Sam and Rusty say hello to Patch.

"Come on, Patch," says Sam. "We'll show you all the animals on our farm."

4

Usborne Farmyard Tales

# THE SILLY SHEEPDOG

### Heather Amery
### Illustrated by Stephen Cartwright

Language Consultant: Betty Root

There is a little yellow duck to find on every page.

# This is Apple Tree Farm.

This is Mrs. Boot, the farmer. She has two children, called Poppy and Sam, and a dog called Rusty.

First they look at the hens.

Patch jumps into the hen run and chases the hens.
They are frightened and fly up onto their house.

"Now we'll go and see the cows."

Patch runs into the field and barks at the cows.
But they just stand and stare at him.

6

Then they look at the pigs.

Patch jumps into the pig pen and chases all the pigs into their little house.

# Sam shouts at Patch.

"Come here, you silly thing. You're meant to be a sheepdog. Ted will have to send you back."

They go to the sheep field.

"Look," says Sam. "One sheep is missing." "Yes, it's that naughty Woolly again," says Ted.

"Where's Patch going?" says Sam.

Patch runs away across the field. Ted, Sam, Poppy and Rusty run after him.

# Patch dives through the hedge.

Patch barks and barks. "What has he found?"
says Sam. They all go to look.

Patch has found a boy.

The boy pats Patch. "Hello," he says. "I wondered who bought you when my Dad sold his farm."

# The boy has found a sheep.

"There's Woolly," says Sam. "I found her on the road," says the boy . "I was bringing her back."

The boy whistles to Patch.

Patch chases Woolly back through the gate. She runs into the field with the other sheep.

Ted stares in surprise.

"Patch doesn't do anything I tell him," says Ted.
"You don't know how to whistle," says the boy.

# Patch runs back to them.

"You must teach me how to whistle to Patch," says Ted. "He's not a silly dog after all," says Sam.

First published in I992 by Usborne Publishing Ltd. Usborne House, 83-85 Saffron Hill, London ECIN 8RT Copyright © Usborne Publishing Ltd. I992